A
KINDNESS

A RICHARD JACKSON BOOK

By Cynthia Rylant

PICTURE BOOKS
All I See
Birthday Presents
Night in the Country
The Relatives Came
This Year's Garden
Miss Maggie
When I Was Young in the Mountains

"The Henry and Mudge Books"

Henry and Mudge
Henry and Mudge in Puddle Trouble
Henry and Mudge in the Green Time
Henry and Mudge Under the Yellow Moon
Henry and Mudge in the Sparkle Days

STORIES
Children of Christmas
Every Living Thing

POETRY
Waiting to Waltz: A Childhood

NOVELS
A Kindness
A Fine White Dust
A Blue-Eyed Daisy

A KINDNESS

Cynthia Rylant

ORCHARD BOOKS • NEW YORK & LONDON
A division of Franklin Watts, Inc.

Copyright © 1988 by Cynthia Rylant. All rights reserved.
The ten lines from "A Kindness" are reprinted from *The Rainbow Grocery*
by William Dickey (Amherst: University of Massachusetts Press, 1978),
copyright © 1978 by William Dickey

Orchard Books
387 Park Avenue South
New York, New York 10016

Orchard Books Great Britain
10 Golden Square
London W1R 3AF England

Orchard Books Australia
14 Mars Road
Lane Cove, New South Wales 2066

Orchard Books Canada
20 Torbay Road
Markham, Ontario 23P 1G6

Orchard Books is a division of Franklin Watts, Inc.

Manufactured in the United States of America
Book design by Mina Greenstein
The text of this book is set in 12 pt. Aldus
1   3   5   7   9   10   8   6   4   2

Library of Congress Cataloging-in-Publication Data
Rylant, Cynthia. A kindness / Cynthia Rylant.
"A Richard Jackson book."
Summary: Having spent his fifteen years happily alone with his mother,
Chip finds his familiar world threatened when she becomes pregnant, re-
fuses to name the father, and confronts him with his own possessiveness.
ISBN 0-531-05767-4.   ISBN 0-531-08367-5 (lib. bdg.)
[1. Mothers and sons—Fiction. 2. Babies—Fiction. 3. Single-parent
family—Fiction.] I. Title. PZ7.R982Ki 1988 [Fic]—dc19
88-1454 CIP AC

✕

Because even if it is not true, I need
something now to look back to, in order to say:
I have been sudden in the sun's perfection,
I have had blood rise like light,
my hands have answered,
my memory is a bush of grown flame.

It is a kindness you can do me, to have been there
at the center of summer, yourself the attack of summer,
and to have made all that light out of being young.

I need to have loved you. I need to have told you so.

WILLIAM DICKEY
from "A Kindness"

ONE

×××
××
×

1

Iᴛ ɪs not difficult to imagine the life of a boy who has lived only with his mother. First, you imagine that he must know her very well, at least those habits of hers by which she creates her days. Second, you imagine that he must feel at once both protected and protective. Protected because he is, after all, not her one child alone but her one family as well, and the single focus of her attention. Protective because being this, being a "one" in any person's life, brings with it a sense of responsibility, a sense of ownership, a sense of power which cannot be experienced in a relationship diffused by brothers or sisters or husbands.

And third, you imagine that the boy and his mother must be alike in many ways, so their differences must be more potent, more acute, than those between two people whose connection is pruned and influenced by others who are living with them.

And so it was with Chip Becker and his mother, Anne.

Fifteen years they had lived together. His father, an ex-hippie, had not been able to muster much interest in a wife and new baby. He lived somewhere in Australia now, leaving the two of them to work out all that must be worked out between a child and his parent.

Chip was brighter than his mother. His was a logical and quick mind—practical and mathematic. He was a computer maestro, spending hours on original compositions of color and design. He was also, in a word, handy. He had assembled all his own Christmas toys as a child, reading lengthy directions in small print on thin paper as his mother stared helplessly at bags of colored pieces of plastic. At eleven he fixed the Hoover vacuum, and at thirteen he filled out Anne's income tax forms.

And for the last two years, every Sunday night he had price-compared in the Acme, making a deal with Anne that if she cooked whatever he bought, he would save her twenty dollars a week.

It worked.

Chip was often perturbed by his mother's impracticality, but he knew it had kept him fed and clothed. She was an artist, and her days were spent in a studio with large windows that let her see out on the back yard of the apartment they rented, a yard full of birds and squirrels and wild rabbits.

And it was this yard, really, that was for them a meeting ground. Because for all the differences between them—the struggle between his pragmatic and her intuitive self, between his concrete and her abstract—they shared one common conviction: a commitment to living things.

Besides the wildlife they kept fed and fat in their back yard, there were tuna-fishing petitions to sign, anti-vivisection bills to support, salmon migrations to follow. There were the cranes in China, the seals in Canada, the coyotes in Wyoming, the manatees in Florida. They each cared, deeply, about extinction, and when the last Dusky Seaside Sparrow died, they had not been able, at all, to speak about it.

Anne had settled in Seattle when Chip was born, and for that he was happy. He loved Washington mornings and the smell of the harbor and the rain. Anne volunteered at the aquarium every Thursday, and, because of that, he had followed the lives of its penguins and sea turtles and sea otters. He kept journals about his favorites.

It had been a sacrifice for Anne to stay in the Northwest when the art world she had known was in New York, and the artists with whom she felt an intimacy continued to live there.

She talked about her New York friends often, and Chip was aware that she missed them. She would, he knew, move back when he finished high school.

But she said New York was no place to raise a child. He'd been born in Seattle, his father's hometown, and because it was beautiful and fresh, she had stayed to raise him there.

And once a year, she fed that longing inside her and went back to New York for a few days to see her friends.

But she satisfied another longing, too, with these trips. Her dealer was there, running a small gallery, and though she could have mailed her paintings to his address as other artists would, instead she carried them in hand to his door. His name was Benjamin George.

Ben.

His name was a familiar one in their house. When paintings were sold and Anne went dancing through the rooms, pink and happy, it was Ben's name Chip had heard in the excitement. Ben who had made the connection, Ben who had stood firm on the sale, Ben who would be sending a check. It was Ben they toasted with ginger ale before they sank their teeth into the biggest celebratory shrimp money could buy.

It was a strange thing for Chip, to feel a sense of debt toward a man he had never met, a man who was only a voice on the telephone, an address on an envelope.

It was a strange thing, to feel safe because of a stranger.

It was a strange thing, to live with the name of a man he had not seen.

And it was, eventually, a strange thing that Chip did not think of the name of the man he had not seen when everything went crazy.

SHE had loved him for years. Nearly everyone who knew her well had known it, except her son. She wasn't ashamed of the love, was very easy in it and content to let him have his happy marriage and good children and grow older and older and never with her. It was all right.

He had not loved her back. At least, not in the way a man could, if he wanted.

They worked together, but across a distance. They lived in different states and the telephone was their only connection, until once a year *they would meet, the work bringing her to his city for a few days. He would tell her how nice it was to see her again, missing the look in her eyes as they sat across a table from each other or moved in and out of a cocktail party like quiet ocean fish.*

She would have gone on loving him until one of them died, and her son would never have known, if not for the tragedy.

The tragedy was that one of the man's good children disappeared. His daughter, a pretty college girl who was depressed for reasons too vague or shameful to tell, dropped out. Vanished. Don't try to find me, she said on her way off the edge.

And the man was shattered. Could not work. Could not eat. Could not see his wife or his other children, only his shining daughter in his mind. The pain of her leaving settled in his chest like a many-edged rock, sharp and unyielding. And it was that pain he brought to the once-a-year meeting with the woman who worked with him, who loved him, and who had a son who did not know this.

Once again they sat across a table from each other. But this time the talk was not so much of work as of the vanished daughter. The man's pain reached out from him as he spoke, and with the words, the reaching, he felt a terrible loneliness, an unbearable loneliness, and this the woman recognized as her own.

It is a powerful intimacy that occurs in the presence of suffering.

For a night she loved him as she always had. He loved her as a man can.

And she took her secret home.

IT WAS October when Anne revealed it.

Chip was in tenth grade and in love with Jeannie Perlman. They had begun dating during the summer and, before either of them was quite prepared for it, had fallen in love.

Jeannie was everything Chip admired—liberated and funny and political and creative. She made jewelry. Her hero was Margaret Sanger. Her ambition was to teach in Central America.

Chip's ambition was to marry her.

So when he opened his eyes and looked at the

glowing hands of his clock that dark, crisp morning, it was Jeannie whom he immediately thought of.

Four-fifteen a.m. What was it?

He lay quiet a moment, feeling his nostrils harden with the sting of cool air coming through his window. He waited. Then he heard it again.

His mother was in the bathroom, vomiting.

Chip rolled out of bed and, shivering in his underwear, went to the bathroom door.

"Mom, you okay?"

From inside, Anne's voice was weak.

"I'm okay, Chip. Just an upset stomach."

"Need anything?"

"A keg of Pepto. Go back to bed. I'll be fine soon. It's just a virus, I think."

"Okay." He walked softly back to his room and curled into a tight ball beneath his comforter. He could hear the pigeons murmuring to each other under the eaves of the building, and at that moment he wished Jeannie were lying beside him, listening to their voices with him. He lay awake a long time, imagining Jeannie's long hair on his pillow and waiting for the sound of Anne returning to her room.

In the morning when he went into the kitchen, Anne's face was pale and her brown eyes wide as moons.

"You look like hell," he said, smiling.

Anne smiled back. "Thanks a lot."

"You think it's the flu or what?"

"What."

"Well. Thank goodness. Now we can relax. I know there's a bottle of what pills around here somewhere." Chip offered her the carton of orange juice. "Want some?"

Anne looked back at him without speaking.

He chuckled. "Right. Yeah." He stuck it back in the refrigerator.

"So, do you need a ride to the doctor? Want me to call Randy or somebody?"

Anne shook her head. "I'll be fine. Don't worry about me."

She sipped her tea and looked out the window toward the bird feeder in the yard. But her eyes seemed not to stop there, and instead traveled deeper and further past the feeder, the trees, the yard. Deeper into some place he could not see.

AT SCHOOL, over lunch, Chip told Jeannie about Anne's illness.

"Maybe I ought to call home," he said, shoveling a piece of pizza into his mouth.

Jeannie picked an olive out of her salad.

"Sure, why not?"

"Well," he answered slowly, "I don't know. I don't want to be a classic Jewish mother." He could feel some sensation creep up on him as he spoke. Some feeling he could not name. "I mean, I don't want to start wringing my hands over her vomit or anything."

Jeannie laughed. "Definitely not."

"So," Chip said, needing to change the subject. "You want to do something tonight? Want to come over and see my program?"

Jeannie shook her head.

"Sorry. Can't. I'm meeting Tom Messinger at seven."

Chip sat up straighter.

"Tom Messinger? Tom Messinger? Why?"

Jeannie gave him a fierce look.

"What, am I supposed to enter this for your approval?"

"Well, no, but . . ." The feeling again. Right on the edge of his mind. He could not name it. "No. You're not. But, hey, I'm supposed to be worried. I'm supposed to say *Tom Messinger*? God made boyfriends to ask questions and repeat names."

He got up and raised his arms to the heavens. "TOM MESSINGER?" he cried dramatically.

He sat down.

"Cute," Jeannie said. "Somehow I missed that decree in the Ten Commandments."

"It comes under the Covet clause."

"Right." She resumed eating her salad. Chip watched her as she ate. And ate. And ate.

"*Well?*" he said finally, throwing up his hands. "Are you going to tell me or what?"

"What."

"I can't believe it," he said. "That's the second time today somebody did that."

Jeannie sighed and pushed her long brown hair away from her face. The silver moons hanging from her ears sparkled and, for a moment, Chip could think only of those, and her skin, and the taste of her lips. For a moment, he forgot everything but that.

"You want to know?" Jeannie said, anger skimming her voice. "I'll tell you. Initially I'd planned to meet Tom at the library at seven so we could work on our death penalty debate for Speech class."

Chip left the sparkling moons. He heard her. He began to speak.

"However," Jeannie said, before he could respond, "since you are being such a jerk, I've changed my mind. Instead, I'm planning to take him out behind the library and perform unspeakable acts on his body." She gave him a direct look. "Just so you won't be disappointed, you understand."

She's so beautiful when she's hot, Chip thought. He grabbed her hand and squeezed it.

"Okay, okay," he said, smiling. "It's just that Tom, he's a real piece of meat around here. And rich."

"Oh, yeah," answered Jeannie. "Just my type. For a minute there I forgot I only want meat and money."

Chip kissed her fingers. "Sorry. I'm jealous, you know."

He narrowed his eyes and bent his head toward hers.

"I vant to possess you," he moaned in his finest Karloff. "I vant to seal you in my dungeon."

Jeannie gave him another look of exasperation.

"Because, my dear," he leaned across the table and put his nose against hers, "you are one fine ball-and-chain."

Jeannie sputtered.

"Hey." Chip leaned back in his seat and rubbed his hand over his face. "You spit in my eye."

And so his day continued, and the odd sensation

left him, went out the back of his spine and into another place, and he was happy and things were right and life was as he wished it.

When he arrived home after school, he found Anne in the kitchen again, eating saltines and sipping a cup of tea.

"So, how's your day been, Mom?" he asked her as he pulled a carton of milk out of the refrigerator. "A little green around the gills?"

Anne laughed. "Definitely a colorful day in the bathroom. How was your own?"

"Oh, my day in the bathroom was great."

"Very funny."

Chip sat down with a handful of graham crackers and a glass of milk.

"I've had these after school every day since I was six," he said. "When do people graduate from crackers and milk to Scotch on the rocks?"

Anne nibbled the saltine. "When they figure out they had a rotten childhood and everything's their parents' fault."

"Oh." Chip grinned. "Well then, I'll put the Scotch on your VISA, okay?"

They sat quietly a while, with their respective crackers and thoughts. Silence for them had never been a dangerous thing. It meant peace, not the war it could mean in other houses. Silence was safe and slow and only when it was gone, only when Anne needed a "talk" about a problem between them, did Chip feel its weight and loss. He hated talk that was required of him.

The phone rang.

"I'll take it. It's for me." Anne headed toward her bedroom.

"What?" Chip called after her. "Got a new boy-friend or something? Kitchen phone's not the right color?" His mother's door clicked shut.

He went back to his crackers and his ruminations about Jeannie and Tom Messinger. How will I get through this night? he wondered. How can I think of anything but Tom's hands moving through that long, dark hair, moving against that light brown neck under those sparkling moons? How can I imagine anything but unspeakable acts behind the library? Probably this is what makes a man ready for Scotch at the end of a day. . . .

Anne stayed in her bedroom a long time, her tea growing cold on the table.

"Mom?" Chip finally called. "You still on the phone?"

No answer.

"Mom?" He got up. For a split second he could

see her in his head, crumpled on the floor of her room, dead from the virus which an autopsy disclosed instead to be cyanide poisoning.

He knocked on the door.

"Mom, you okay?"

Her voice shook as it came through the wood.

"I'm okay."

"Mom?" Was she crying? "Mom, what is it?"

He waited. He heard her blow her nose.

"It's all right. Come on in."

He turned the knob, running a list through his head of everyone they knew who could have died.

Anne sat on the edge of the bed beside the telephone, mounds of tissue lying beside her and clutched in her hands. With the dark curls against her head and the condor shirt she was wearing and the stuffed toy gorilla propped against her pillow, she seemed to him, suddenly, a child.

"Mom? What's happened? Did something happen? Who was it? Is somebody . . . ?"

"No." Anne wiped her nose and shook her head. She took a deep breath. "Everyone's okay."

"Well, you're not," he said.

"Right."

Part of him didn't want to be in that room. Part of him was floating out, floating out through the cracks around the windows and through the ducts and out the door. Part of him did not want to say what he said:

"Is there anything I can do?"

Anne sighed. "Just hear me a second."

"Okay." He sat down in the wicker chair across from the bed and waited, and floated.

"This is going to be hard." Anne's mouth trembled and her eyes filled up again.

Chip braced, holding back any feelings, taking no chances.

Anne cleared her throat, inhaled, and forced out the truth:

"I'm pregnant."

Her body shivered as she said it and the chill crossed the room and passed into her son.

His eyes widened, his arms fell limp, and he went dead. It was not what he expected. Ever.

Anne went on, calming as more words came.

"It's not Randy, of course. Nothing's changed with him. And I know you must wonder . . . I haven't dated in a long time. But who it is isn't important. And where and when and why is my business anyway. The bottom line is that I'm pregnant and I'm a little wiped out about that but things will be okay, Chip. They will be."

Now the sensation was with him again, and as he felt it traveling along his spine, crawling into his stomach, flooding into his head, he finally recognized it as fear.

She said it again and more firmly: "Things will be okay."

And he thought, Thank God. His head settled.

"Gosh, Mom, you really had me scared. For a minute there I thought you were going to tell me you had cancer or AIDS or something."

Anne chuckled and blew her nose.

"Whew," he said, feeling on top of it finally. "Pregnant is easy. I mean, not easy, but treatable, right? Things will be okay."

Each was silent. He wanted to ask her: *Who? When? How could . . . ?* But there were things to take care of.

"Listen, Mom," he said finally, "I don't know how you feel about this, but if you want me to help you . . . I mean, like go with you . . . when you, like, go to the clinic or wherever they do them, I'd be happy to drive you and wait and . . ."

Anne's head turned toward his and at that instant he felt locked into something so powerful, something so certain and strong, something so inescapable, that he shut up.

"Wait," she said, looking into his face. "Wait. I'm not ready . . . I don't know if I can . . . Chip, it's not that easy, and right now I'm so numb that I can't think, but I know I can't just decide right here not to have this child. I know I need to give . . ."

"*What?*" Chip gawked at her. "You mean you might *have* it?" It was too much to comprehend. "Are you *serious?*

"What about me, Mom? Have you thought about me and how I might feel about my mother suddenly walking around *pregnant?* This isn't just your problem, Mom. It's mine, too. This is *my* business, too."

They looked at each other. Chip was shaking now, his face flushed, his arms and legs weak. But Anne had grown steadier. Her eyes had dried and her mouth was firm.

"*Your* problem?" she said quietly. "Your business? Yes, Chip, you'll be affected if this baby is born. . . ."

"It's not a baby yet. It's a thing."

Anne went on. "But what led to the conception is my business, the news I got today is my business, and what I decide to do about it is my business. I will not, hear me, *not* make this decision based on your wants or your anger or your fears. It's my life here. You'll be gone in a few years anyway, and I'm not about to choose based on what you want for your life, Chip. My life is not yours!"

And he stopped then. Stopped the fight. Stopped the talk. Stopped the listening. Something too painful was happening. Something too hard.

He pushed away all the words with his hands, pushed them into the walls and the floor and the furniture. Pushed them out of his head and stomach. And without looking at her face again, he left.

3

How MANY boys ever have to face the losing of everything? Boys in war-torn countries certainly. Boys in the third world.

But a comfortable American boy who has no bombs from which to run, no threat of starvation to face daily, for him the losing of everything cannot mean, in a practical sense, those things tangible like limbs or life itself. For him it can mean only beliefs. It can mean only the falling away of everything he is certain of and has faith in and relies on never to be altered.

What Chip had become certain of was that he would be his mother's only child. What Chip had had faith in was that he knew who she was. And what he had relied on never to be altered was the life they had created for themselves over fifteen years.

He rode his bike through the dark, wet streets, his face glowing white and green and blue from neon lights, the red reflectors on his spokes spinning around and around and around with his thoughts.

There was something ugly in it he did not trust himself to regard. Something ugly in the truth she had told him.

When had it happened? Who was she with? Why did he not know this part of her?

Who *was* she?

He pedaled hard, working away at his anger like a block of granite, letting himself be consumed by the physical so the emotional would not rush in to swallow him up.

He biked mindlessly all over the city and finally, wet and exhausted, he called Jeannie.

"I have to see you."

"Chip, it's ten-thirty. Where are you anyway? I hear traffic."

"At a 7-Eleven. Jeannie, I really need to talk."
It had come to this for him. His body would endure
no more and as the feelings seeped in where the
adrenalin flowed away, he knew there could be no
silence for him. No peace in silence. He was ready
for words; he needed a talk.

"Chip, if it's about Tom Messinger, I can tell
you right now that . . ."

"No. It isn't that. It's me. Please, Jeannie, I need
to see you."

"Okay. I'll tell my parents you're coming. I
hope it's that important because they will be mildly
teed this late."

"It's a crisis, Jeannie."

When she opened her front door, and he saw
her eyes and her mouth and her soft, warm body,
he realized how incredibly deserted he felt.

"You look like death," she said.

"I feel it."

She took his hand and led him into the den. Her
parents, tactfully, remained upstairs.

Jeannie propped her elbow on the back of the
sofa and faced him.

"What is it?" She asked the question as if it
were a mathematical problem. No drama. No shrill
edge. He hated the tone, but it calmed him.

"My mom," he said, looking down at her hand. "She's pregnant." And on that last word he could feel his throat closing up just as Anne's must have five hours earlier.

Jeannie took a quick, deep breath.

"But who . . . ?" she started to ask.

"Pick a number," he answered. And after he'd said it, such a hard, hard thing, he quickly raised his head and found her eyes. When he did, his own flooded.

"She might have it," he whispered.

"Really?" Jeannie's voice was a whisper now as well. "With no . . . ?"

"Right. Father. Can you believe it?"

Jeannie sighed and remained quiet. Chip waited, heavy and tired.

"I can believe it," she finally answered. "Anne really cares about things, you know. She's just like you that way. Good grief, the way she worries about those animals at the aquarium . . ."

"Yeah," Chip said, "but they're *animals*. This is a nothing so far. Some cells. Some stupid tadpole. And she's going to blow *everything* for it."

"Maybe."

"She will. Watch her."

He was trembling all over now. Even his teeth
he couldn't keep still.

Jeannie pulled the afghan from the back of the
sofa across his shoulders.

"Gosh, you're really upset about this."

He nodded his head.

"I know it's upsetting," she said, smoothing
back a lock of the blond hair which had fallen across
his eye. "But why are you in such *hell*? I mean,
it's not you. It's not us."

He just shook his head.

"Why, Chip?"

He moved through all those words in his head,
crowds and crowds of words that could answer her,
but there were so many and every one screamed
so to be said that he could not say any of them.

A tear rolled down his face as he shook his head
again.

"Do you worry what people will think? Is that
it?"

He nodded. The words fit.

"Is that all?"

He knew it couldn't be. There had to be more,
more than that for all the pain.

"Things will be . . . different," he said finally.
"At home."

"Right. A screaming kid and diapers and poop

and noise and . . ." He let himself be lost in the madness he envisioned.

"Taking care of it," Jeannie finished.

"Right. I don't want to take care of a stupid kid, for pete's sake. I don't even like kids that much. You ever see them yelling their heads off in K-Mart? Who'd want one of those in his house?" He looked at her. "Would you? Would you want one of them hollering upstairs right now?"

Jeannie smiled and shook her head. "No thanks."

"I don't know . . ." He could feel the crowd of words thinning, the faces of words becoming visible. "It's going to screw up my entire life if she has this kid."

Jeannie straightened up. She took her hand away from his.

"Aren't you kind of exaggerating things there, Chip?"

He watched her face.

"I mean," she continued, "Anne's the one who has to go through it, not you. She's thirty-five and always practically broke. Her job with you is nearly over and just when she could be getting ready to fly like a bird, she's got *another* one growing in her."

Jeannie put her hand to her forehead. "Good

grief, what she must be feeling right now. There's no good answer. Either way, she's going to get hurt.''

Chip heard the voice, the sound of Jeannie trying to reach him, but his gut could not connect. It was too soon, and he was too . . . *appalled* . . . to feel any sympathy for Anne right now.

So he simply sat. And Jeannie could see that what he needed was only that, to sit. She pulled him toward her and laid his head on her shoulder. She kissed his ears, the back of his neck, his eyelids. And she held him for a long time.

WHEN HE finally arrived home near midnight, Anne was in bed and only a small lamp in the living room burned.

He turned it off and sank into a chair in the dark.

His mind would not let him feel the pain he needed to feel, so his thoughts became a carousel of practical arguments.

Two bedrooms, he thought. Only two bedrooms in the house. If she had it, where would it sleep? Not in his room. Not on your life. With her? He couldn't imagine it. But then, he couldn't imagine any of it. Everything would be a nightmare. She'd get fat and slow and crabby. The place would go to pot. And he'd have to get more than just lawn jobs to help buy the Pampers. Forget college. Forget Greenpeace. Forget . . .

Then he stopped and realized, fully, that after all, the kid had a father in town somewhere, snoring away while Chip sat with all this load.

Who is he, anyway? Maybe he'd take it. If they hauled him into court and proved Anne couldn't feed two kids. Who is it? Somebody at the museum? A Mystery Man.

And I'm no fool, Chip thought. Mystery men are always *married* men. The guy won't want the kid. He'll probably even deny that it was him who . . . did it.

Maybe she'll fall. Not enough to hurt herself. Just enough to jolt it out.

And it is an *it*, he told himself. Just some cells and muck.

"It's not a kid," he whispered to the darkness. "It's nothing."

For that night, Chip believed in nothing. It was all he could do.

WHEN he finally called her, she knew she was carrying his child. Seven weeks had passed since they'd been together. It was time enough for a baby to have a beginning.

He spoke of his child, but not, of course, the one which grew in her. The child he talked of was his daughter, the vanished daughter, who had been seen in Greenwich Village and whose sighting had renewed in him hope that he would find her and save her and bring her home.

And Anne listened, with every second won-

dering when he would move from the daughter
to herself and to him and to what had happened
between them.

She gave him time—she was good at that—
and finally he did come to it. It was difficult for
him, she knew, to discuss that for which he
would suffer much guilt and regret. He had gone
back home to his happy marriage, and the night
he had separated himself from that marriage he
needed to relinquish.

But he could not relinquish Anne. He cared
about her. And there was the work. So he made
a try at repairing the injury. He made a try at
friendship and forgiveness and a future.

But the pain of that try was for Anne worse
than the pain of his not loving her at all. She
wanted not to be something he must mend. She
wanted nothing from him except to avoid the
humiliation in that.

So to save what she could, she asked him for
time away, time without contact. She asked him
for a year, and though he protested and asked
for compromise and effort and patience, finally
he did agree because he heard in her voice a
hardness he was unused to and did not know
how to soften. He promised to refer her to

someone else with whom she could work. He promised to be back.

When the phone was returned to its cradle, and he was gone, the tears she had fought away dropped wet and hot from her eyes. She lay on her bed and wrapped her arms around her pillow, curled like a child. She held the pillow and imagined it was him. Imagined his smell, the sweet taste of his mouth, the heat of his breath. She remembered the things he'd said to her through the night.

She had not stopped loving him. And those things which she had said to him through the night and which were still alive in her, she would not give away. She had no regrets, and she would not give them away.

4

A WEEK had passed since Anne told Chip her truth, a week of hollow words. An easy silence in the house was impossible, and their mornings had been filled with the words you hear in elevators and on airplanes and at church socials. They were the words that edge the surface of feelings and revelations the way water bugs skim the tops of dark lakes. Words between strangers. Even enemies, in comparison, are more intimate.

Anne's sickness continued, making it difficult for Chip to allow the rage in him to take shape. He listened to her vomiting in the bathroom in the early morning hours and was lacerated with guilt. He offered her no help, no concern, and the pain of that, the hardness of it, was like a fire in his stomach. And yet as he listened to her with this fire and offered nothing, at the same time he felt a kind of pleasure, and even hoped she would vomit *everything* up, and that would be the end of the problem.

She had not made a decision. This infuriated him as well, since it tapped into an old history. She had never been very good at it, making decisions, and as far back as Chip could remember, Anne had bungled and stumbled until *he* made the choices for her. Even trivial things like where to go out to eat she had not been able to decide. Or more weighty matters like whether to stay home or travel away at Christmas.

She had left so much in his lap. But this was one decision she couldn't dump his way, and he felt a new lightness in that, a freedom, even though he would have been happy to tell her what she could do with the whole mess.

On Friday night their friend Randy arrived for the ritual linguine dinner he had cooked at their house once a month for nearly ten years. Randy was not Anne's lover. Nor was he Chip's substitute father. He was an antiquarian bookseller and a saxophone player and a friend, and there were no blurred boundaries in this. Randy was clear. For the first time, Chip realized how grateful he was for that, for this man who at least held no secrets, no surprises, no fogs. And Chip knew Randy couldn't be the Mystery Man because of this clarity.

Chip brought Jeannie for dinner, and they came through the door just as Randy was dumping a pot of hot noodles into the colander.

"Yo!" Chip hailed.

"Hey, brother," said Randy, squinting in the steam.

Anne stood at the counter, chopping up a green pepper. She smiled at Chip, who avoided her eyes.

Jeannie walked over to her.

"Need some help?"

"No thanks." Anne threw the pepper pieces into the salad. "That's the last of it." She wiped her hands on a dishtowel.

"How're you feeling?" Jeannie asked gently.

Anne caught her eyes and blushed.

"To be honest, about like that linguine over there," she said with a grin. Randy was holding a wet noodle above his mouth, ready to drop it in.

"Oh. I always identify with linguine," Jeannie answered. "No breasts."

Anne laughed and gave her a hug. Chip watched them and felt he'd like to hug Anne and club her at the same time. Then he wondered if all the stress was starting to crack him up.

Once the four of them gathered at the round table, though, and eased into that familiar rapport of people who know each other in ways which are precious, and apart from the rest of the world, his emotions evened and he could forgive his mother for a time.

But during one particular moment when Jeannie had said something funny and Randy was howling and Anne was dabbing her watering eyes and the four of them were *tight* and *solid*, Chip saw what was happening, what was really happening and what his life was, and he thought, If she has this kid, this will be finished. We'll have a Mickey Mouse high chair squeezed in there and mashed carrots all over the wall. Cookie Monster will be hollering for more Oreos and the smell of pee will make us all delirious.

And he hated the threat to his life as he knew it. And even more than he wished to punish his mother, he wished to punish the man whom she had been with and who would lose nothing for it.

After dinner, they sat on big pillows in the living room, playing Trivial Pursuit. Naturally, Chip was a whiz at it and Anne a dismal failure.

"Who *cares* what leafy crop is Cuba's second-biggest export?" she groaned.

"The world cares, Anne," Randy said. "Vanna White cares. Sly Stallone cares. Madonna cares." He snapped his fingers. "This is the Trivial Generation and it's leaving you behind."

"Okay, Randy." Jeannie drew a card. "Your turn: What two mountain ranges does the Tour de France race through?"

"The Pyrenees and the Alps," he answered without hesitation.

"Right!" Jeannie yelled.

"I don't believe it," muttered Anne.

Later, after Chip won the game and the five dollars Randy had bet against him, they lay around the room with cups of hot cider, talking. Randy propped himself against the stereo, while Chip lay on the sofa. Anne sprawled across the armchair, and Jeannie lay on her stomach on the floor.

"I am so full," Jeannie grumbled.

"Maybe the linguine will go to your breasts," Chip answered.

"Fat chance," she said.

"That's what I meant."

Randy smiled at them, then looked at Anne. He knew that she was pregnant. She had phoned him the day she found out, the day Chip had run out of the apartment. Chip had been gone for hours when she called Randy, hoping he might know something of her son. She would not call Jeannie's house, wouldn't embarrass Chip like that. Randy had calmed her, assured her the boy just needed time alone and would be all right. Anne would not tell Randy the name of the man she had been with. Randy knew, though. There was only one man she loved enough to protect. And while he couldn't imagine it happening, couldn't imagine Ben allowing himself the experience of her love, he knew that what he could not imagine happening had happened. And that what she faced was not just a decision about having a baby, but a decision about having Ben's baby.

She looked tired. He was sorry for her. And for Chip. And for Ben, though not for reasons connected to the child. He was sorry for Ben that he probably would have only one night with a woman like Anne.

She's loved him for years, Randy thought.

The evening stayed drowsy and warm until ten-thirty, when Randy had to leave for his gig. He offered Jeannie a ride home but Chip wrapped both his arms around her neck and challenged Randy to steal her from his clutches.

Randy grinned at Jeannie.

"I guess that means no thanks."

"Guess so." Jeannie grinned back.

Chip snorted in triumph.

So Randy left and Anne went to bed and Chip and Jeannie cleaned up the kitchen. Chip loved being with her like this, passing pots back and forth as they talked about everything from favorite candy bars to Supreme Court decisions. He loved watching her reach to the top of the cabinets, the curve of her body as it stretched, the tightness of it. He loved the way her hands moved under the running water of the sink. And the way her hair fell across her eyes each time she bent over, the way it got between her lips. And her lips. Just her lips.

When they were finished, they burrowed into each other in the corner of the sofa and kissed. Chip could feel that rolling coming through him, that stampede of sensations that covered him each time he was with Jeannie like this. Sometimes he felt he was drowning in it and he got frightened and had to say something funny to stay above it.

But tonight he wanted not to stay above it but to sink, to be swallowed, to be inside the thunder so no thoughts could reach him, no troubles. And he nearly made it, nearly lost himself in the love, until, kissing the hollow of Jeannie's throat, feeling her hand move along his thigh, he suddenly wondered what it had been like when his mother and the man had . . .

And he slung that thought away like a snake.

Yet, this night, there was no drowning for him because of it.

5

A<small>NNE HAD</small> already made her decision before that night of linguine and Trivial Pursuit. Perhaps she was inept when it came to choosing between fast-food restaurants, but with the issue a child taking hold in her womb, Anne would not allow herself the risk of whirling confusion. She realized what time meant; she became more finely aware of its control of her life than ever before. Time no longer was the limbo she painted her way in and out of each day. It was no longer measured in large pieces, in decades or eras, as she had always preferred it, leaving clocks and watches to those whose work was counted in lengths of nine-to-five or forty-hour.

Time suddenly meant to her the shaping of fingers. The emerging of ears. The budding of teeth. The forking away from animal to human.

It meant for her a visible line which, if crossed over, would rob her of any choice at all.

And so she could not shrug time away. She could not play her games with it.

She could only confront it, unwavering, and acknowledge its power, and make her decision.

She would have the baby.

It was a sea turtle named Ulysses that helped her.

On Thursday, Anne's usual day at the aquarium, she had been assigned the task of watching Ulysses for two hours and making notes on his behavior for the marine biologist. It was an assignment she accepted gratefully, for she'd had little sleep the night before and still fought the nausea that came over her in unexpected surges. She pulled up a folding chair beside the turtle tank, took a deep, relaxing breath, and gave her eyes to Ulysses.

He was the youngest turtle of the four in the tank, and his youth was evident in his speed and his frisky inquisitiveness. He was only ten years old; the oldest turtle, Sappho, was nearly eighty.

Anne watched Ulysses and, perhaps because she was tired or because she had lately been intensely thoughtful, she could not maintain the clinical detachment needed to note subtle behaviors in an animal.

Instead, as she watched the turtle sweep past her with his large peaceful eyes searching the coral and the movements of his comrades, she thought about where he had come from.

Sea turtles are egg-laying animals, and the females come ashore during their lifetimes only to bury their eggs in sandy beaches. The eggs rest there, and provided they are not ravaged by humans or predators such as ghost crabs, they hatch after a few weeks.

The baby turtles must dig themselves up out of the sand and find their way into the sea, or they will die of dehydration or attack. Few of them survive. And those who do make it into the water then become easy prey for larger ocean animals or diving birds.

Ulysses, Anne knew, had been one of the thousands of baby sea turtles who claw their way to the surface of the sand and who defy every odd by searching out the brightest horizon and crawling across a vast beach under the hot sun toward that water which will mean life for them.

Anne watched Ulysses' eyes and wondered on which beach he had fought for his life. He was one of the baby sea turtles who had miraculously survived, who had struggled to escape the death which would seem certain for a creature so helpless in an environment so hostile.

And as she watched Ulysses swim, and loved him for his fight and his victory, Anne realized, in one searing instant, that to give up the baby that had a start in her would be, for her, like giving one of those baby turtles over to the hot sun or the preying crabs that hunted them.

In her gratitude for the grace which had allowed Ulysses to survive, Anne was stunned by what possibilities waited in her womb. And being the woman she was, the woman who fought the extinction of animals as if it were a personal threat to her own existence, being this woman, she saw, finally, that she could live only with one decision: to have the baby.

There on the folding chair, she watched Ulysses with tears streaming down her face, grieving for everything she knew she would lose so that a life could turn toward the brightest horizon.

CHIP did not know of Anne's decision that day because she was too afraid to tell him. In all their years together, he had never seemed so full of hate for her. The hate crippled her and caused her to lose sight of her strength as mother, as adult. It weakened her and staggered her so that she could not tell him on Thursday evening or Friday morning or Friday afternoon the choice she had to make. And so, for those twenty-four hours, one lived by fear and the other by anger, and the baby that stood between them through no choice of its own developed fingers.

But Saturday morning, nine days after she had faced her son with the unexpected truth, Anne awoke resolved to tell him what their future held.

She walked into the kitchen, where he sat eating a bowl of cereal, and asked him for a talk.

"Okay," he said, dropping his spoon into the bowl and pushing the bowl away. He was very tired this morning, tired of the effort required to punish someone, the energy demanded to blame relentlessly. He was drained and nearly ready to give it up.

"First," Anne said, sitting across the table from

him with her fingers clasped, "I need to say I love you."

"Okay." He would not look at her.

"And I'm sorry that we've both been through so much this past week."

"Okay." He knew what must be coming. He knew she'd made a choice. And he tried to brace himself, to be ready for whatever he heard. He wished only that she'd do it fast. Get to it, he thought.

And as if she knew he needed this speed, Anne said it:

"I'm going to have the baby."

Chip's shoulders slumped. He shook his head.

"I can't believe it," he said, even though, deep in him, he really could. It really was what he'd expected. But he needed to say those words anyway. He needed to act this thing out.

"Well, believe it," Anne said. Her stomach hardened for the fight she felt coming. "Look, we can't keep arguing over this. We can't just keep wishing it hadn't happened. The reality is I'm having a baby and the truth needs to be faced and lived with."

"Truth?" Chip exclaimed. It was exactly the word he was looking for. He knew how to use it. "*Truth?* The whole thing's a lie! You sneak off with who knows what man, you get knocked up, you won't tell who he is or bring him into it, you're lying about whose business it is. What truth?''

And for Anne, Chip said exactly the word she was looking for. It was as though they were fencing with rehearsed moves and tipped rapiers.

''Whose *business* it is?'' she repeated. ''It is *not* your business, Chip! Yes, the father won't be involved, but I refuse to share the reasons with you because they are *none of your business.*''

She flushed. ''And don't think you're going to make me feel like a slut. That's one power I'm not giving away to anybody.''

Chip seemed not even to hear her. He was ready with the rest of the lines he needed to say, lines he'd been saving.

''I can't believe you think you even have the right to have a baby!'' he yelled.

''The *right*?'' Anne could not believe the rage she was feeling toward her own son.

''Yeah, the right. You brought one kid into the world with a turd for a father. Now you're going to have another kid who won't even get that much. Not even a turd for a father!''

''The choices your dad made were his, Chip. I'm not taking the blame for his choices.''

''Yeah, well you're not taking the blame for

much of anything, are you, Mom? You're sitting there *pregnant* and you're not taking the blame for much of anything. Well, here comes one more kid with no father. Congratulations. It's amazing how you keep writing the same old story but you still act like somebody else made it up.''

He was very good with the words. Anne could feel the tremors in her arms and legs.

''I didn't know,'' she said, her voice quiet, ''that you hated it so much, having only me.'' Her hands gripped the edge of her chair in an attempt to stop the trembling.

''Yeah? Well, sometimes I do! Sometimes I'm just tired of your being so stupid. Sometimes I just want you to have some answers. I want you to know things like other normal people. But then, you're not normal, are you? You never have been. And it's been me who had to figure it all out, make it work, keep it running. You were too busy in la-la land to see that there were things that had to be *done*.'' Chip's heart pounded and he was afraid the words might kill him. It was as if they had a life of their own, and he heard them and feared them and felt powerless to stop them. He watched Anne, too, to see if she might die because of them.

But she did not die. She did not evaporate. She

sat silently, looking at him with wet eyes, her shoulders shaking, and she remained steady and alive.

Chip saw this, and he knew the rage had found its way to her and that now, with it exposed and freed, he could be quiet. He could talk.

"I don't want to take care of a baby, Mom," he said, looking out the window. "I'm fifteen and I don't want it."

"What makes you think you'll have to?" she asked, confused.

Chip's head turned back and his eyes met hers.

"Are you kidding? I take care of everything. I've taken care of *you* for years."

"What?" Anne seemed to be floundering. "What?"

"I *had* to!" Chip's mouth shook and he could feel the terrible grief that he wanted to dam begin to push against him. "Who else was there? You wouldn't get married again. You wouldn't find somebody."

"I didn't want anyone!" Anne tried to catch up with and go beyond what he was saying. She wanted time to think about it, but there wasn't any. "That's what *you* wanted, Chip. You wanted it and I didn't know why."

"Because then I wouldn't have to worry!" He ran his fingers through his hair. His knees quivered. "Because you didn't have anybody but *me*. Nobody but me at Christmas. Nobody but me at Thanksgiving. Nobody but me morning and night. God, I used to worry I might *die* and you'd have NOBODY!"

Anne sobbed then, at this revelation she had never guessed. She had not known.

"I didn't know," she whispered. Chip had begun to cry. He buried his face in his hands and for several minutes there was only the sound of his sorrow.

Finally Anne got up and brought back to the table a box of tissues. She took a handful and passed the box to him.

"I'm sorry," she said, sighing deeply. "Somehow I let the boundaries get blurred without realizing it. You were never responsible for me, you know. You were never responsible for making me happy."

She shook her head. "I should have told you that. I should have guessed how you'd feel, being the only one here."

Chip, too, sighed and leaned back into his chair. There was a peace now, a kind of giddiness, and he felt a crazy urge to laugh.

"I need to have this baby and I'd like to keep your love," Anne said gently. "I don't need your help in taking care of it and I don't need your presence to keep me happy or safe. I have no expectations of you. I just ask that you not punish me for the way I have to live."

Chip sighed again. He blew his nose. He rubbed his eyes. Then he looked at her with a small reluctant grin.

"You never liked kids, you know," he said.

"What?" Anne exclaimed, grinning back.

"You never liked Kool-Aid or station wagons or Rice Krispie treats or the P.T.A. or . . ."

"Well, I still liked kids! I liked *you*!"

"I do admit you were great at Halloween."

Anne chuckled. "My butterfly costume."

"Right."

Both were smiling now, relieved to have survived each other's words, and feeling for a moment safe again in that home. But the future, each of them knew, was not safe and could not be trusted. Little in their lives could be trusted.

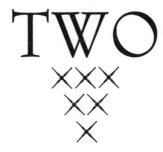

and look her in the eye and
owardly piece of slime you

let you feel it kick. It kicks
w. It's already got a hell of a
than you.

it. She sits in her rocker every
she sings old Beatles tunes to
Back and forth, back and forth.
girl or should I say she once
k and forth.

is look about her, too. She's like
n almost feel it coming off her,
is. All the plants in the house
and fatter than ever. I think it's
g my zits, this energy she's
f.

ering whether it's a boy or girl?
essing girl. I don't know, maybe
shing it. A girl will handle it bet-
ving a dad. You jerk. She'll key
those female things Anne does,
ow and then—like at grade school
the kids tell where their daddy
ill she feel she's been cheated.
embarrassed about it—count on

can come back
admit what a
are.

Maybe she'll
all the time no
lot more guts

She sings to
morning and
her stomach.
"I once had a
had me?" Bac

She's got th
shiny. You ca
whatever it
are greener
even helpir
throwing of

You wond
Well, I'm gu
I'm just wil
ter not ha
right in to
and only r
when all
works—w
She'll be

What
computer
ing it, yo
She's gett
little seed
ing and it'

She stop
didn't hang
much puke
now so you

TWO

XXX
XX
X

6

What I'd like to tell you, **Chip typed on his computer one day in March,** is that you're missing it, you sucker. You're missing all of it. She's getting prettier and prettier and that little seed you planted keeps right on growing and it's incredible and you're missing it.

She stopped throwing up. Is that why you didn't hang around for the encore, jack? Too much puke for you? Well, she smells okay now so you can come back if you want. You can come back and look her in the eye and admit what a cowardly piece of slime you are.

Maybe she'll let you feel it kick. It kicks all the time now. It's already got a hell of a lot more guts than you.

She sings to it. She sits in her rocker every morning and she sings old Beatles tunes to her stomach. Back and forth, back and forth. "I once had a girl or should I say she once had me?" Back and forth.

She's got this look about her, too. She's like <u>shiny</u>. You can almost feel it coming off her, whatever it is. All the plants in the house are greener and fatter than ever. I think it's even helping my zits, this energy she's throwing off.

You wondering whether it's a boy or girl? Well, I'm guessing girl. I don't know, maybe I'm just wishing it. A girl will handle it better not having a dad. You jerk. She'll key right in to those female things Anne does, and only now and then—like at grade school when all the kids tell where their daddy works—will she feel she's been cheated. She'll be embarrassed about it—count on it—that there's no daddy to speak of to the teacher. Even I know who my real one is but he's so long gone I had to make everything up. Said he was a geologist exploring for oil in Australia. He'll be back for Christmas, I'd announce. But the teacher never asked whether or not he came, when Christmas rolled around.

So she'll feel plenty bad those times, you ultimate turd, but she'll get through it. And she'll do the things with Mom I hated to do. Like eat in restaurants. Shop for clothes. Sunbathe. And that'll be good.

Who knows whether or not she'll like the animals at the aquarium. She's got some of your degenerate genes in her so I wouldn't be surprised if she left the sea turtles to fight their extinction on their own.

But I'm hoping not. I'm hoping Anne and I can strain those nauseating traits of yours out of her quick, so she won't grow up and do what you do like an art: sneak out the back door.

What I'm wondering is, Who are you? Except for Randy, there hasn't been a man around here for a long time. So which rock did she find <u>you</u> under? Are you some Norwegian sailor who pulled into the harbor for a night? Some lumberjack down off Mt. Hood? Did your eyes lock on her across some bar and you said to yourself, "This one's gonna be easy"?

But we both know Anne doesn't bar-hop. She hates that game. She doesn't hit singles clubs or body shops or yuppie parties . . . so where'd she get <u>you</u>?

Hell, if I didn't know better, I could almost believe in immaculate conception.

You interested in me? Wonder what the Boy's like?

Well, I'll tell you: I'm loyal. Know that word? I make commitments to people and I keep them. I don't do anything I can't live with the next day. I scope things out. I pick and choose. I think about the future, turd.

Today I've got a mom who's six months pregnant with <u>your</u> kid and today I'm thinking about the future. Today I'm painting the bedroom that used to be Anne's purple. She's going to sleep in her studio—not too romantic so I guess she isn't expecting you to drop by anytime soon. Purple is a good color for a baby, I figure. There's going to be a streak of buttercup yellow running right through the middle of it like a Georgia O'Keeffe painting:

Future nursery.

Today I'm looking for summer work even if it's only March because the way I figure it, the new kid is going to cost us a cool couple of thousand and unless Ben does some incredible song and dance in the next three months, we ain't got it:

Future finances.

Today I'm talking to my girl Jeannie about sex and contraception and all that stuff because Anne's condition has got Jeannie so uptight that it's getting so I can hardly touch her anywhere but her elbows and she's running:

Future platonic relationship.

Today I'm watching my mother sing to a stomach and choke down fried liver and forgive the gossiping neighbors and laugh at the bulge she's growing and sit in her rocker in the dark in the middle of the night looking out at harbor lights and thinking and thinking and thinking while she lets something grow that's going to hurt her and trap her and punish her. Right. Punish. Because the kid's going to grow up and when she's about, say, fifteen, she's going to look at Anne and she's going to shout, "What made you think you had the <u>right</u> not to give me a father, anyway?"

Future peacemaking.

Today I'm imagining what that baby's going to be like. And I see nothing but a blur. Some doofus-faced Gerber ad that slobbers and screams and poops and costs money. Great.

But I'm not as limited as you, schmuck. That's not all I see. I see this little girl, too. And she's picking out the scrawniest Charlie Brown Christmas tree on the whole lot because that's the kind of kid she is and it would be a hell of a world without the ones who come along picking up the scrawniest Christmas trees.

I see this girl who might paint pictures like Anne's.

I see this girl who might search and search to the ends of the earth for another Dusky Seaside Sparrow even though we <u>told</u> her they're all gone and we <u>told</u> her it's a waste of time to look, but she goes looking anyway and somewhere in a dense Canadian forest she finds TWO!

And the two will be as one and they'll have a baby Dusky and the daddy sparrow won't go sneaking out the back door.

Know what I wish for you, jack? I wish you'd go searching like Don Quixote, chasing those windmills but always feeling this big hole inside you. And the hole gets bigger and bigger and pretty soon it's eaten up your liver. And pretty soon after that it's eaten up your kidney. And you're still chasing those windmills. Pretty soon it's eaten up your lungs. You're still chasing those windmills.

And pretty soon, it's eaten up your heart.

And just when it's all gone, that heart, you'll see her:

You'll see Anne on the street and she'll be walking with this beautiful little girl with curly dark hair and their faces will hold everything you've been chasing after all those years.

But you'll have no heart to offer them.

And pretty soon, you die.

You're missing it, sucker.

7

When the baby began its journey to the brightest horizon, it was five in the morning. Anne woke up to find her sheet soaked with the amniotic fluid the baby had decided to be free of, and she called Randy. Then she called her doctor. Then she made herself a cup of tea and filled the bird feeder on the windowsill. Then she woke Chip for school and mentioned that it had begun.

Having babies is like having colds to those whose hearts are not directly involved. But if you are a boy whose mother, whose only parent, whose only family is about to give birth, then see what happens. You replay in your mind every scene from every old movie you've witnessed in which a woman lies in agony in a dimly lit room, screaming and clutching the mattress with white knuckles as lumpy village women murmur beside her and exchange knowing looks that she isn't going to make it. You see the doctor softly closing that bedroom door behind him, the doctor's eyes turning to the woman's husband who waits outside, the doctor's head giving a mournful shake. You see the unspeakable despair which crosses the poor husband's face, you see him take hold of a table or chair to steady himself. You see the terrible finality of it all. . . .

"I'm coming, too," Chip announced at the kitchen table.

"You are not," Anne answered. "You're going to school."

"But I *want* to come, Mom."

Anne smiled. "So you can explain the workings of the fetal monitor to the obstetrician or the mysteries of an epidural to the anesthesiologist?"

She shook her head and patted his hand. "Thanks, but I'll have as many experts as I can handle. Besides, they'll just make you sit in the waiting room and watch *Wheel of Fortune*."

"They wouldn't!"

"Count on it. Only my Lamaze coach gets to stay."

Chip grinned. "I bet Randy is going *nuts* right now. I bet he's already gone through three packs of cigarettes and ten cups of coffee since you called."

Anne chuckled.

"I bet," Chip continued gleefully, "he's flipping frantically through that Lamaze book and he's puffing and gasping and choking, trying to remember when to breathe, forgetting *even* to breathe, and he's hyperventilating, and you'll have to take a cab to the hospital because Randy's passed out on his kitchen floor in a dead faint, with a Camel in his mouth and a fat pillow between *his* knees instead of yours!"

And with that they laughed hysterically, their faces bright red and tears streaming and noses running and it was very likely a good thing for a baby to hear.

So Chip went to school, with a frozen chicken casserole in the refrigerator waiting, and a purple and yellow nursery with ten boxes of Newborn Pampers waiting, and a suitcase packed with nightgowns that read "0 months" by the front door waiting, and a mother who occasionally bent over slightly with pain as she counted her way in and out of a minute, waiting.

At ten o'clock in the evening of that same day, the baby was born.

Anne had told Chip he could name the child when it came, so the following morning he carried a handful of roses and a stuffed panda and a name to the hospital. When he walked into Anne's room, she was sitting up in bed sipping orange juice through a straw and he couldn't decide whether she resembled a child or an octogenarian. She wore a white gown with pale blue stripes, and a plastic bracelet on one wrist.

Chip looked at the bracelet.

"I guess they didn't want me to mix you up with someone else's mother and take her home by mistake."

Anne laughed. She looked tired.

"I can't believe it's a girl," Chip said. "I was right."

Anne smiled and nodded.

"When did Randy leave?"

"About midnight. First he had to play with the baby. She probably imprinted on him like a duck and . . ."

"She'll follow him around for the next eighteen

years saying, 'Are you my mother?' " Chip finished with a laugh.

"So . . . how are *you* doing?" Anne asked him.

"Oh, not bad," he said, grinning. "I slept maybe two hours last night."

"Sounds like you needed my anesthesiologist."

"Right."

Both were quiet.

"Randy told me her eyes are blue."

"They are. But they might change."

"And that she's got black hair and looks like a little troll."

"He said *that*?"

Chip laughed.

"He said you were great, Mom."

Anne blushed and shrugged her shoulders.

"Except for when you called him that name."

"What name?" Anne asked. Then her eyes got wide. "Oh. *That* name."

"Too bad to repeat here. They'd blooper it."

"Well, I was hurting like hell and I didn't want *anybody* and he reached over and . . ."

"Forget it, Mom. You're forgiven. By me anyway. Randy, he's suing you for a couple of million."

Anne giggled as the woman in the bed next to

hers looked on in wonder, unable to decipher the connection between these two.

Chip gave Anne a shy grin.

"You ready for the name?" he asked.

"Sure." She smiled. "Somebody asked me what her name is, and all I could say was it's probably somewhere on a floppy disk."

It was Chip's turn to blush.

"Her name," he said after a ragged deep breath, "is Dusky Anne."

Anne stopped smiling. She stopped breathing. And he immediately thought she hated the name he had chosen.

But then her eyes began to flood. And one by one the tears came out like timid children. And he knew it was all right.

The baby wasn't yet due in Anne's room for a feeding, so Chip decided to walk down to the hospital nursery to see her. Anne offered to go with him, but he said no. He wanted to be alone when he and Dusky met.

He went out into the hall, carrying the panda, and past the nurses' station, around the corner, and down another long hall to the nursery at its end. On his way he passed room after room of women in bathrobes, some with husbands or mothers beside them, but more often alone. He saw these women in their flowered robes and pastel slippers and he thought it an odd thing, an eerie thing, that there were no babies in their arms. Each could have been any woman, any patient. No one could know, passing their rooms, hearing the game show hosts crow on their televisions, that, only hours before, their bodies had opened wider than anyone might reasonably imagine and a human being who had never been seen had come out of those depths. He marveled that Anne, his own mother, had just experienced this, and there were no traces of it on her.

He had imagined lovemaking many times before, had thought of how two people could be together in ways too amazing to dream, and the following morning someone could look at them and see no visible traces of what they'd experienced.

What he expected to see he did not know. But for so profound an internal change, he could hardly believe the absence of an external one.

When he came to the large window of the nursery, other people were there. He noticed the faces of the men who stood with their smiles pressed up against the glass, and he felt a pain in him for Dusky, having no dad to look at her.

He took a deep breath, pushed his blond hair out of his eyes, tucked the panda under his arm, and looked in.

He found her right away, in the basket with the pink bow marked "Becker." He found Dusky Anne Becker, and she was awake.

Randy's right, he thought. A troll baby. Her fuzzy black hair stuck straight up. Her eyes were large and wandering. Her nose was flat and red.

It's a living, breathing Ewok, he said to himself.

He mashed his nose against the glass with the other men, and for a long time he stood there at her window, Dusky Anne's, wondering who she would be.

8

"THE KID'S driving me nuts," Chip told Jeannie over lunch two weeks later. "You can't imagine the lungs on her. I bet that's what they grow first. First the sperm hits the egg. Then the egg hunkers down in the womb. Then the egg grows a pair of *lungs*. And when the kid pops out after nine months of waiting to use them, first thing she does is scream for two entire weeks."

Jeannie gave him a look of mild tolerance and bit into her hamburger.

"That bad, huh?" she said with her mouth full.

"Bad? *Bad?*" Chip shook his head. "Hell hath no fury like a new baby, let me tell you."

"It'll improve," Jeannie said.

"Right. When she's eighteen."

"Chip!" Jeannie glared at him. "Do you *enjoy* all this moaning and groaning?"

He gave her a sour look and bit into his own hamburger.

"So. How's Anne today?" Jeannie asked.

"Tired." He couldn't mention that his mother hadn't painted anything in four months, that he missed the smell of the oils and turpentine, that he wished she still emerged from her studio with paint in her hair and her eyes glazed. He couldn't tell Jeannie how he worried that Anne might stop painting altogether. He was too afraid to say it aloud.

"And how are you then, oh Master of the Monosyllable?"

"Ugh," he said.

"As I thought," she answered.

Chip grabbed her hand.

"You know what I need?" he said with a sly grin.

Jeannie raised her eyebrows.

"The universal lament of the male species," she answered.

"Give you three guesses."

Jeannie grinned reluctantly. "I probably don't need them, but I'll bite."

"You *will*?" Chip's face lit up. "That's just what I need! Right here." He pointed to his throat. "Oh, not a large bite. A small one would do. Just a little hickey I can call my own."

Jeannie's grin began to weaken, but Chip gave it no notice. He took her other hand.

"Jeannie," he said softly. "It's been so long since we had a good . . . neck."

"Sure you don't mean it's been so good since we had a long neck?" Her serious eyes betrayed the easy response, but still Chip was not connecting.

He smiled and leaned toward her.

"Jeannie . . . love." He lowered his voice. "I promise. No funny stuff. No babies. The last thing I want is another Dusky. But I miss, you know, how close we could get. Don't you miss it?"

Jeannie's face grew serious.

"I don't miss the scariness, Chip. I don't miss the worrying that some night we'll forget or we'll go insane or something and next thing we know we're at some clinic. Because you *know* I wouldn't be as noble as Anne if ever . . ."

"Anne's not noble," Chip interrupted. "It didn't have anything to do with noble. You make her sound like a saint."

"What are you so edgy about?" Jeannie pulled her hands away from his. "Just because I used a word . . ."

"The wrong word." Chip slumped back in his chair. "And I'm not edgy. I'm just saying she's not a saint."

Jeannie was silent.

"What?" he said. "What is it?"

She shook her head.

"*What?*"

"Chip, when are you going to give up this role of defining who everybody is? You know, it's amazing how you just sum up somebody with a few words. You do it with your mom, and you'll do it with me, wait and see. You'll start saying, 'Jeannie's not this, she's *this*.' And that really scares me."

Chip looked at her, bewildered.

"I don't know what you're talking about," he said.

Jeannie pushed back her chair and stood up, tray in hand.

"I know," she answered.

And without even a goodbye, she walked away. And when he called her to stop, she would not look back.

Watching her leave him, Chip realized that unconsciously he had been preparing for this. Since Anne's pregnancy had been announced, Jeannie had begun changing in subtle ways. She had become very busy, having meetings to attend, friends to study with, work to do. He had hoped she would help him paint the nursery—a romantic experience, he thought—but suddenly she began a new piece of jewelry and pleaded too much involvement with that. So he'd painted the room by himself.

Then in the last few weeks of Anne's pregnancy, Jeannie had practically disappeared altogether. She spent most lunch hours in the art room with an oil painting she said she was obsessed with. She wanted to date only when they would be among a group of people. And the night Dusky was born, she was out and didn't even return Chip's call when she came home.

He knew he was losing her. But he had been willing to deny that, sidestep it, bury it for as long as he could.

Until this day, when she walked away.

She had pushed him away from her, literally, so many times in recent weeks, as they were kissing and touching. Jeannie had always been so open to it—the touching, the exploring, the loving. But lately she had withdrawn without explanation, and he was so afraid she didn't love him anymore that he could not ask her why.

And if he had not been in such an abyss as he watched her walk away, Chip might have understood that it was not the absence of love but the presence of fear controlling her. Fear of the choices she would always have to make when she was with him.

But he could see only what was: that the girl he loved, her back to him, was leaving. He sat in the cafeteria, the din of voices like a steady machine in his head and he wondered if Jeannie really had stopped loving him. And then he went further: he wondered whether he was worth loving at all.

At the end of the day, that which he had most dreaded, most feared, waited for him.

Slipped through the vent of his locker, the note read: "Dear Chip, I don't think we should see each other for a while. It's getting too serious for me. Too heavy. Maybe if we just cool things, we can work it out later. You just get so intense and I don't want intensity right now. I'm really, really sorry. Love, Jeannie."

Chip crushed the paper in his hand and tossed

it into the trash. Then he took his pain and loneliness home. Home to a place which, a year ago,
would have provided some solace and safety but
which now was simply a place of chaos. The clean
small kitchen table he had loved to sit at was now
full of the strange pots and pans of Anne's friends
who had brought food. The quiet intimate air of
the apartment he had known was crowded with the
voices of too many people, coming in and out.
Ever-present were the cries of an infant he neither
wanted nor liked. And always missing, among
everything, was the mother who had nothing to
give him now and who once had everything to give
him.

For the rest of the day he sat in that place, watching all this go on around him, because he could
not move himself to find a different place. He was
so numbed that he could only sit and watch Jeannie
get up and walk away, again and again, in his mind.
He had given up on everything and there was nothing in him that said get out, get moving, get busy,
get happy.

But late that evening, past midnight, he was
forced out of his inertia.

Anne became ill. Her vomiting began at about
one a.m. and it was clearly serious. It would not

stop, even when her stomach had expelled all it could. Chip held her up over the toilet bowl as she retched, and they knew they were in trouble.

"Call Randy," she said, gasping, tears in her eyes.

And within minutes Randy was there, and out the door with her, and Chip was left holding Dusky in a dark, empty hallway.

The baby had awakened, though she was not yet crying, and she was soaked. She searched against Chip's chest to nurse, and even in the dark with no one there to see, he was mightily embarrassed.

He carried her into the nursery to change her diaper and clothing.

Every time he had changed Dusky's diaper he had laughed, and even tonight, with Anne traveling to an emergency room and his feeling of utter loneliness, he still laughed.

Girl babies were just so *different* from boy babies. Oh, he knew this logically and practically, but . . . visually and emotionally he just had not experienced the difference until he changed a diaper.

The first time he'd unwrapped the Pamper and looked, he was startled, and what immediately popped into his mind was Mr. Potato Head. Dusky looked like Mr. Potato Head without his nose. Chip thought it the silliest thing he had ever seen.

And now, every time he changed her diaper, he remembered Mr. Potato Head's missing nose and he laughed. Even this night, this worst of nights.

Dusky was hungry, and before he had a clean, dry gown on her she was wailing. Her cries made him panic and he fumbled and could not get her arms into the sleeves of the gown. Looking about him frantically, he saw hanging in the closet a snowsuit one of Anne's friends in Alaska had sent Dusky for next winter. It was big enough for three Dusky's but he dumped her into it anyway.

Bouncing her on his shoulder as her screams rattled his brain, he went into the kitchen to warm a bottle. It seemed an eternity until the milk was ready, and he tried to keep calm, to breathe deeply, though by the time he flopped into the rocker with the bottle and baby, he was shaking all over.

He had fed Dusky a bottle only once before, and that was in the middle of the day, with his mother looking on.

He'd never been up in the middle of the night with the child. Anne had made it clear she did not want his help in that. In fact, she rarely accepted any help from him. She seemed intent on releasing him from the caretaking he had been doing in their home.

So it was not surprising that being completely alone with a newborn baby in the dead of night was affecting his nerves.

Somehow, though, he had gotten it right, and Dusky accepted the bottle and his arms.

And it was in this moment, in this time, that Chip began to love the child.

As she nursed, he sang to her. He sang what he thought she'd like: the mockingbird song. And while she sucked and cooed to her bottle, he looked at her, really looked at her.

He examined her fingers, little lined old-woman fingers. He looked at the lashes that lay on her perfect baby skin. He felt her ears. He leaned over and smelled her hair.

When she turned her head from the bottle, satisfied, he placed her on his shoulder as Anne had taught him and he patted her back, singing some more. She let go two wonderful burps which made him smile. Then she turned her face into his neck, and she breathed her new, warm, milky air on his skin and slept.

When Randy and Anne finally returned—she medicated for food poisoning—they found Chip and the baby in Chip's bed, the tiny crop of Dusky's black hair just beneath his chin, her face hidden deep in the snowsuit he enveloped with his arms.

That night, Chip owned a baby. And it was that fleeting ownership which would draw him to the man he had not met, and did not know, and could not forgive.

9

Ben did not wait a year.

When Dusky was three months old and finally sleeping through the night, he called.

Anne and Chip were eating a pizza in front of the TV news. Anne was not prepared for Ben. She'd thought at least another month remained to rehearse what she had to say to him and to strengthen herself to do it.

But he did not wait.

When she picked up the kitchen phone and heard him, her face went ghost white. Her breathing grew shallow, her voice dropped, her body stiffened, and the son who watched her from the living room knew—because he was smart and because he listened to his gut—that Dusky's father was on the line.

And as if replaying a familiar scene from an old movie, Anne said to Chip, "It's for me. I'll take it in my room."

He watched her leave the kitchen.

She called behind her, "Will you hang it up in there for me?" And her door clicked shut.

Imagine that you have been searching for someone for nearly a year. Imagine that you don't know his face or his voice or even his name. You have lain awake nights, staring at the ceiling and drawing pictures of him in your mind. Some nights he is tall and blond. Other nights he is short and dark. Some nights he is young, barely past adolescence. Other nights he has grandchildren.

There have been mornings when you leave your apartment building half expecting him to be watching you from the curb across the street. You have looked behind your back more than once in the grocery. You have sorted through the day's mail with slightly sweaty hands.

Imagine that you hate him so much you wonder

whether you will be struck dead for such hate. Imagine that you fear him more than any disease, any plague.

You are a boy obsessed with a phantom and it has been like a chunk of lead in your heart, this obsession.

And one night, while you are eating pepperoni pizza in front of the evening news, the phantom is there. He is waiting on the phone while your mother goes to pick up the other extension.

Chip stared across the room at that receiver as Anne left it on the counter. It was like staring at a grenade ready to blow. He rose and walked over to it. He reached out and picked it up.

"Anne?" he heard the phantom say.

And he hung up the phone.

He stood with his hand still on the receiver as his mind was wiped clean of everything but one word: *Ben.*

That voice had been a part of his childhood, his life. He knew it well, though he had never met the man whose voice it was.

Ben.

He could not fathom it. Ben had never been *human* to him. He had been the other end of a check, that's all. He had been a basket of fruit at

Christmas. He had been a tax-deductible number on a telephone bill. He had never been a *man*.

And Ben was already a father! He was *married*, for God's sake. Chip knew all the stats on him: house, wife, kids, dog. He knew him.

And one night nearly a year ago—and yes, it *was* in New York as Chip had eventually come to suspect—Ben and Anne had . . . made a painting. Her name was Dusky.

Anne had done a very good cover-up on him, mentioning casually months ago that he was going to Italy for a long stay, that someone else would be handling her work until he returned.

It explained everything. It had made so much sense, seemed such a natural thing, that Chip had not once been suspicious. He bought his mother's lie because it was *too* natural, *too* real, and all along he had been searching for the unnatural and the unreal.

The phantom was Santa Claus, and Chip had never figured Santa to do anything but send checks.

Their conversation was brief and Anne emerged from her bedroom within minutes. She was upset and he knew it, though she tried desperately to hide her feelings. With a lightness like tin in her voice, she mentioned that the caller had been Ben. Chip simply nodded his head.

They returned to cold pizza and the comforting drone of television, and when Dusky woke up with a cry, each jumped, grateful for the distraction.

It was Chip who went into the nursery, who walked through the purple room to the baby in the bed. When Dusky saw his face, she smiled and kicked her legs.

"Hi, Booper," he whispered. He lifted her up and held her tight against his chest. She fit against him easily now, as if each had learned the contours of the other and knew where to lay a head, fix a shoulder, wrap an arm.

Chip put his lips to the baby's hair, smoothed his cheek against her forehead, hummed to her the mockingbird song.

And he realized he was *terrified*. Because he had always known that a sailor or a lumberjack would never come looking for this baby. A one-night man would never come for this child.

But Ben. Ben was an owner of things. He owned a business. He owned a house. He owned a wife. He owned children.

And Chip believed he would accept nothing less than owning Dusky.

Chip stood in the powdery room, summer light cutting across it, and he swayed back and forth with the baby he loved as terror crept its way through him. There was nowhere to run. He couldn't go to Jeannie. Nor could he take his fear to his mother. He had accepted long ago that Dusky's father was a subject Anne would not, under any amount of pressure, discuss. Chip had always thought she'd hidden the man out of shame. Now he realized she probably meant to protect the man, to protect Ben.

But who would protect Chip? Who would protect him from the power of a man who could come into this apartment, this nursery, this *life* he lived with his mother and Dusky and alter everything?

Dusky began to fuss, straining against his arms, so he carried her to Anne, then went into his room while she nursed. Anne's breastfeeding was one of those natural acts he could only retreat unnaturally from.

In his room he sat on the edge of his bed, stiff and trembling, searching in his head for a place to take his terror.

And he finally thought of Randy.

He told Anne he was going to a friend's house, then headed his bike toward Randy's used bookstore. The shop closed at seven, and it was nearly half-past, but Chip knew that sometimes Randy stayed in late to work. And he knew that if he didn't catch him at the store, he wouldn't find him, because Randy always ate out and rarely was home long enough to do anything except check his mail before going to his gig.

"Be there," Chip whispered into the air.

As he wheeled nearer the tiny shop and saw the familiar green shade of Randy's desk lamp aglow through the window, his body relaxed. He would be all right, in there.

He tapped the window that read "Archer's Used and Rare Books." He saw Randy lift his head, then a large smile cross his face. And finally, Chip was inside.

"Yo," Randy said easily, hands inside his pockets.

"Hi." Chip stayed beside the door. He looked around nervously.

"What brings you here?" Randy asked, eyebrows raised, eyes soft. "Trouble back at the ranch?"

Chip sniffed and grinned. "Yeah."

Randy gestured toward his desk.

"You take the chair. I'll take the stool."

Chip dropped into the chair as Randy pulled a footstool from behind a shelf and slid it next to Chip's feet. Randy squatted down on it, his knees almost to his chin.

Chip started out of his seat. "Listen, I'll take the

stool and . . ." But Randy stopped him with a hand on his arm.

"Stay. I'm fine." He propped his elbows on his knees, put his hands together, leaned forward, and said, "What's wrong?"

And before he had any sense of what was happening, Chip's eyes filled up. It had been so long since anyone had looked at him this way, with such gentleness, such interest. It had been so long since anyone had asked him in these troubled months, *"What's wrong?"*

Randy waited quietly as Chip calmed himself and wiped his wet face.

"I know who it is," Chip said with a tight voice.

Randy said nothing.

"It's Ben," Chip finished.

Randy drew in a deep breath.

"Anne finally told you?" he asked.

"No." Chip shook his head. "But I know. Believe me, I'm right about this."

Randy gave him a long look.

"Yes," he answered, nodding his head. "I believe you are."

"You knew?" Chip asked.

Randy shook his head. "Only in the way that you know. She never told me."

Chip gave a hard sigh and his eyes looked away into a corner.

"God, I miss Jeannie," he said.

Randy smiled. "You're keeping me from dinner to *miss Jeannie?*"

Chip grinned.

"No." He hesitated, his face becoming serious again. "I'm just scared."

"Of what?" Randy leaned forward.

"Him."

"Ben."

"Yeah," Chip answered. "I'm scared he'll want Dusky."

"He might. But he'll have to share her with you and Anne."

"I don't *want* to share her!" Chip said fiercely.

Randy's eyes widened. He shook his head, rubbed his beard.

"You're giving yourself a lot of power, my friend." He paused. "That child's life does not belong to you."

And Chip suddenly heard those words again, those hard words of Anne's that he had run wildly from nearly a year ago: "My life is not yours!" And he knew, *knew*, he had done it again. He had taken possession of something that did not belong to him, never knowing he'd done such a thing. He laid his head back and looked at the ceiling.

"Damn," he muttered.

Randy smiled and reached across to take hold of his shoulder.

"It'll work out," he told him. "Whatever happens you can deal with, and you won't lose anything you need if you just stay tuned to what's yours and what's theirs." He shook his head sympathetically. "Brother, this is one time in your life when you don't have to take care of other people. Use it, man. Give 'em up."

Chip smiled.

"I'll probably have to move to the Arctic to do it."

Randy laughed. "I don't know," he answered. "Hooking up with a nice girl would be a hell of a lot more convenient."

Chip blushed. The possibility of that excited him, and it freed him in a quiet, powerful way.

"Want an egg roll?" Randy asked.

"Sure," Chip said. "One question, though."

Randy waited.

"How come you and Anne never . . ." Chip began.

"Whoa!" Randy stood up. "What's yours and what's theirs. This one, Chippy, is theirs."

Chip shook his head and grinned.

"Right. Sorry. Forgot."

Randy locked up the store then, and Chip put an arm across the man's shoulder and followed him to dinner.

10

"I KNOW who he is."

As soon as Chip uttered the words, he regretted it. He loathed himself at once, and as he met Anne's alarmed eyes across the top of Dusky's head, he knew he'd started something awful.

"What?" Anne said.

Chip looked away, out, all the way to New York.

"I know who Dusky's father is," he said.

Anne stared at him, unable to speak. Dusky lay asleep in her arms, clutching her blouse with a tiny fist, and Anne instinctively pulled the baby closer.

Chip looked at his mother, expecting her to take control of things from this point, to guide him into revelation. But she could only look at him with her large, frightened eyes and wait for him to finish what he'd so regrettably begun.

And with a hardness in his voice he'd learned from her, he said, "I know it's Ben."

For many years after, Chip would remember what it was like to sit in that room at that moment looking at his mother's face. The August light was cutting across her in that hard yellow slant which is never repeated any other time of the year. That yellow which intensifies every object, every shape in its path so that all seems stunned by it, and at its mercy.

Chip sat in the big blue chair against the southern window. Anne was in the rocker, nearly in the middle of the room, and the summer light came in and held her and her baby inside it. There was no sound except Dusky's heavy sighs of contented sleep. There was no smell except the fragrance of talcum which dominated any room where Dusky was. And the feeling Chip would always remember was his own weak heart pounding through his head as he looked at his mother's eyes, there in the hard-lit room.

"A year ago, right?" he said. "Last August, in New York?"

Anne did not speak.

"I never made the connection." Chip smiled ruefully. "I mean, I should at least have figured out it happened in New York, but I was never really sure."

He could see that Anne intended only to listen. He went on.

"I thought you'd just had a one-nighter with somebody, you know. A quick lay and out the door."

He shook his head.

"I just never figured it was really somebody you knew. And Ben of all people. God, Ben. I'd sooner have believed it was Abraham Lincoln. Ben's always been around here, in our house with us, but never like a person. More like a cash register or a checkbook. It's like you slept with a *checkbook*."

Anne sighed and looked down at the floor, gathering Dusky tighter against her.

"Great conversation we're having here, Mom."

Anne would not look up. He knew he'd walked into a room to which she forbade anyone entrance. She'd told him again and again to stay outside it. And Randy had tried to tell him. But it was as if he were helpless to this voice which *insisted* he cross that threshold and know everything he wanted to know.

For many long minutes they sat there in silence, Chip looking out, Anne looking down, Dusky connecting them as she slept. It was a scene neither Chip nor Anne could have imagined in any way a year earlier. Back then, it was still a life they understood. Chip was with Jeannie. In her heart, Anne was with Ben. But this day it was a life they could never have believed, were they not living it.

There seemed nothing for Chip but to walk around inside the forbidden room, challenge its silence, talk to its unyielding walls. He went on again.

"I can understand two people coming together like that. Really I can. I can see it happening, even if I can't see it happening with Ben."

He leaned back and took a deep breath, focusing his eyes on Dusky.

"What I don't get," he continued, "is how he could just let you go through it all by yourself. How he could just hide out in New York or Italy or wherever and let you go through all this mess and not even once come to see how the baby . . ."

Anne lifted a hand to stop him. She raised her eyes from the floor and looked back at his.

"Because he doesn't know," she said softly.

What Chip did not expect then was the pain he felt when she spoke those words. Why it hurt he could not have said, did not understand really. But the look on her face, the tone of her voice, the solitary shape of his mother sitting in the rocker with a baby she had not been able to give up . . . all that, and the reality that she'd chosen all of it for her life, hurt him terribly. An aching sense of abandonment swept over him, but this time it was not his own abandonment he mourned. It was his mother's.

"I began loving Ben years ago," she said finally, her fingers stroking Dusky's hair. "I think you'd understand, if you met him. I think you'd see right away what there is to love. And then, of course, there was the work. I wanted desperately to be shown in New York, but there were so many painters and too few galleries and even fewer sensitive dealers. I needed someone who would care for my works as if they were alive. It mattered to me where the paintings went, what happened to them. It always has."

Her eyes widened and turned toward the trees outside. She had gone back to that time.

"He saw one of my pieces in someone's home in Manhattan and he called me—out here, you were about five then—and, well, that's what glued it all together, I guess. The art.''

She smiled shyly.

''I went to New York and we met. And I honestly think I loved him as soon as I saw him.''

She stopped, and looked down at Dusky. Her fingers traced the perfect brow, the soft, round cheek.

''He never knew, these years, that I loved him,'' she continued, her voice so low Chip found himself leaning into it.

''And he didn't love me. He was married and I could see that he didn't feel anything for me except that respect and liking that came naturally out of the work.''

She bit her lower lip and looked to the trees again.

''He didn't love me last August either.'' She shook her head gently. ''But somehow, then, it just didn't matter.''

Chip saw her swallow back the tears that pushed at her, saw her fight the loss of composure. He looked away, not wanting to invade her private sorrow.

Anne lifted Dusky and laid her up against her shoulder, allowing the baby's small head to nestle into her neck. She began to rock, gently rubbing her back.

Chip wanted, just then, no more battles. He wanted to let go all of it and be with her in her pain.

But one more thing had to be learned. He must know it.

"Mom," he said quietly, "are you going to tell him?"

Anne's head jerked up and he knew by her eyes she had not made that decision.

"What did you say when he called?" Chip pressed. "Has he figured it out?"

Anne shook her head.

"Well," Chip could feel the frustration shaking him, "you'd better get with it, Mom. I mean, I know you've been trying to protect him and so far it's worked, he's stayed out of this, but . . ."

"Wait," Anne interrupted. "Yes, I did want to protect Ben. But I wanted to protect myself, too. I didn't want the pain of his being here through the pregnancy and attempting to fix everything, to fix everyone's feelings, to do the noble thing while denying that he hated what was happening. Everything I've done has been for my sake as well as his. Believe me."

"Okay. I believe you. But you know he'll want
Dusky if he finds out she's his. You think he won't?
You think he won't come out here with his bag
full of daddy-rights? You think he'll keep his butt
out of our home? No way."

Anne was shaking her head.

"No, he's not like that, Chip. He's not arrogant.
He's *kind*. He wouldn't hurt . . ."

"*Bull*." Chip forced an angry sigh. "He'll be
here."

"Not if I say no," Anne protested.

"Yeah? And will you?" Chip's eyes pinned hers
across the room. "Will you?"

"I don't know," Anne said weakly.

"Do you want him here *now*?" Chip asked.

She shook her head.

"I don't think so. Not right now. Not even for
Dusky. Right now it just wouldn't . . ."

"Then don't tell him Dusky's *his*!" Chip
exclaimed.

But Ben, he knew, would find out soon, somehow, and he would take control of it all. Chip knew
the kind of person Ben was. One owner always
recognizes another.

That night Chip took into his bed Ben and Dusky
and Anne and he lay awake for hours moving them

like chess pieces in his head. He moved them from square to square again and again, himself always the center, never changing position lest he lose connection with one of them.

But Ben was unpredictable as a pawn. Chip would finish a plan and move everyone into place and believe he'd taken Ben off the board, believe he had Anne and Dusky and himself safe, when there would be suddenly an opening and the man was with them again, and immovable.

Chip was still awake when Anne rose in the night to nurse Dusky. He listened to their sounds coming from the nursery and he wondered what their home had been like before Dusky came. He couldn't remember.

He couldn't imagine life without the sounds and smells of Dusky in it.

He wanted not to lose her. But he could not take that pawn.

11

BENJAMIN GEORGE was an intuitive man. He had an awareness he could not explain, only act upon. This gift had made him a powerful art dealer. He knew instinctively who would be great, which artists would quietly and surely paint their way into the very blood of the society. He could search them out, these painters, track them down, and after an exchange of only a few words know exactly what to say to them to inspire them to enormous trust . . . and surprising dependence.

He had known what to say to Anne to keep her

painting all these years. She could have stopped, could have taken a teaching job with predictable pay and circumscribed days, restricted enough to keep her imaginative life safely tethered. She could have gone out the door with Chip every morning, locking her studio behind her, and for eight hours have lost herself in a life of structure and form. Each noon she could have sat in the teacher's lounge, a green plastic lunch tray in front of her, hidden in that safe cameraderie of the workplace. Then with all those hours gone, she could have returned home, deadened, and waited for that day to be over and the next one to begin. Having painted nothing.

It would have kept her safe, that life. Safe in every way, but particularly safe from the visions in the darkness which linger always to be found. Darkness forever terrifying, even to those most gifted.

Ben knew what to say to Anne to keep her facing that darkness, keep her reaching into it for something never seen, never born, never yet imagined by anyone else in the world. Ben knew how to keep her painting and risking everything for that.

But it was a mystery, that all the years they'd worked together he'd never realized Anne was in love with him. Gifted as he was, he also had a protective barrier which he'd never been aware of until Anne revealed her feelings the night they were together. He understood afterward that he had unconsciously barred himself from seeing the part of her that loved him. He had denied that knowledge and was ashamed to realize that it was the businessman working in him. Love is not good for business.

Eleven months after New York in August, Ben had listened to the voice of a woman whom he did not know at all. A woman capable of a coldness which reached out of the telephone like a hand, and he *knew* something had happened to her which had far more power than simply one night of loving him.

And because of that night, and the art, and the kind of man he was, Ben could do nothing else but find out the truth hidden in Anne's new voice.

He had the time, too, for seeking it out, because his lost daughter had finally returned home. She was the reason for his calling Anne a month before their agreed time. He wanted to share with Anne his joy at having a lost child safe in his life again. And he wanted somehow to express how grateful he was for Anne's loving, her tenderness, her willingness to live in his pain for a night.

But the coldness in the telephone cut him short.

And now he had no choice but to come into her life behind her back.

He knew the names of those few in New York who would be familiar with Anne's life. Though they were not personal friends of his own, he had enough connections with them to be able to link himself to their information. And in a week's time he had the truth he sought: Anne was the mother of a baby girl.

Instinctive as he was, this was a revelation he did not see coming, and it hit him like a violent blow. He tried to find out how old the baby was, desperately hoping it would prove not to be his own. But this he could not discover precisely—only that the child was a girl and a few months old.

He knew in his heart, of course, that she was his own baby girl. He wanted it not to be so. But wanting did not change what he knew.

He was lost again, as he had been when his daughter disappeared, and he could not work. He spent days walking the endless blocks of New York, as if he might walk the knowledge away, and in the August city heat this was a punishment, but one for which he nevertheless longed. The suffering he had inflicted on Anne and her son. The suffering he had yet to inflict on his faithful wife and his own children. He could see nothing but infinite pain for all these people whom he had wanted only to take care of.

After several days of confusion and aching, he finally made a decision: he would travel to Seattle to see Anne. Using the work as an excuse would help make it appear a necessary trip, though he'd never gone to her before. He would see her, however, no matter her wishes.

WHEN CHIP picked up the telephone that afternoon, he had expected Randy on the line. The two of them were going to hear a jazz band later that evening, and Randy was notorious for triple-checking arrangements with people.

Chip picked up the phone, his mouth full of cookies, and grunted, "Yo."

The voice was tentative:

"Hello Chip. This is Ben George. Is your mother free?"

Chip was too surprised by the voice of his phantom to respond with anything else but the truth:

"She took Dusky to get her shots."

And suddenly there it was, hanging between

them like a web. Chip heard his own words and immediately wished he could unsay them. Ben could not speak at all for many seconds.

Finally he said the only thing he could:

"How is your new sister, Chip?"

Heart racing, Chip searched for the right tactical response. The game had begun and the pawn waited. But living the moves, the strategy, at long last, was in reality harder than he had ever anticipated, and he could not think.

"Fine," he answered.

"Good."

Ben was silent then. In past years when he'd gotten Chip on the line, he had cheerfully asked how school was, which subjects Chip liked. Today, Ben could not do it.

"Does she have your blond hair?" he asked.

"No, it's black." Chip knew from photographs that Ben's hair, too, was black.

Ben chuckled.

"Dark like her mother's own . . ." he began.

"No," Chip blurted. "Like her father's."

The statement shocked them both. Chip felt possessed, to have said such a thing. Ben simply felt slapped.

Finally Ben regained his position.

"Are they healthy?" he asked, "Anne and . . .
what did you say your sister's name is?"

"They're fine. Her name is Dusky."

"Oh." Ben was quiet. "A pretty name."

Chip was waiting for the man to close this thing.
He wanted not to say more, not to give Ben anything else from their home.

"Well," Ben said, clearing his throat, "I just
called Anne to tell her when I'll be coming out, so
I guess I'll call later and . . ."

"You're coming *here*?" Chip exclaimed.
"When?"

Ben was taken aback by Chip's sudden reaction.
He paused, then said, "Well, I hope to come next
week if I can get . . ."

"Are you *serious*?" Chip nearly shouted. "Are
you freaking *serious*?"

Ben was stunned. He didn't know what was happening, how to respond. For many seconds there
was only a tense silence between them.

Eventually Ben took a deep breath and braced
to meet this boy.

"I guess you know," he said.

"Yeah. I know." Chip was trembling with anger. He wanted to kill the man.

"I'm sorry, Chip," Ben said quietly. "I didn't

know about Anne and Dusky until just recently. I would have helped . . ."

His voice trailed off as he realized how inadequate the words sounded.

"Yeah. Right," Chip said bitterly. "Like bigamy or what?"

Ben said nothing.

"She's better off without your help," Chip said. "So's Dusky. They're both better off without your coming out here where you don't belong."

"But it's my responsibility. Anne can't . . ."

"Bull. She *is*. She's—we're—making it okay and she was just fine till you called her."

"But I have to support my own child," Ben insisted, the strain more apparent in his voice.

Chip gave a bitter sigh.

"Yeah. And tear everybody up."

"I know things won't be easy," Ben answered, "but I'm sure everyone can somehow find a way to live with this."

"Yeah? *How?*" Chip snapped. "Just what sweet little arrangement have you got in mind? Gonna kiss the wife goodbye and hop the plane to Seattle to visit the other woman and the baby you two screwed around and made? Are you gonna just bop out here and say 'Hi, Chip, how's school? Hi,

Anne, how's work? Hi, Dusky, how's life without Daddy?' "

Ben realized he could not talk this boy away. Chip had him.

"Then what'll you want next?" Chip continued. "Us to put little Dusky and her dolly on a plane to New York so she can toddle into your house and feel in her veins how pissed off everybody there is because she was *born*?"

Chip's heart beat hard against his chest and his legs shook out of control.

"How much you gonna make us and her pay so you can consider yourself a good daddy?"

Ben answered in a near-whisper: "I don't know."

"Yeah." Chip paused. "Well."

He seemed then to have exploded all his anger. The quiet was returning.

"I guess you'll do what you need to do," Chip said finally, a sadness in his voice. "I guess you'll do whatever you want."

He gave a heavy sigh, and then, believing himself defeated, hung up the phone.

He left Ben in misery. Chip's quiet agony, the boy's final release of him moved him painfully into a new awareness. And he was shamed toward a decision for the good of all rather than the selfish integrity of one.

The pawn became willing to take himself.

Chip, when the conversation was finished, felt a calm move through him that he did not anticipate. He walked into the living room and sat down in Anne's rocker, looking out the window.

It was nearly September and soon he would be sixteen, driving a car all around the city. He was grateful he hadn't needed to work this summer, that Anne had encouraged him to give this time to himself. But maybe in the fall he'd look for something, some part-time job. Just for him.

He would begin looking at colleges this year, too, for a good marine biology program. And then there was Jeannie. She hadn't dated anyone else since they separated, and sometimes when he looked at her he saw something in her eyes that told him maybe . . .

There was much to look forward to. But with all that, he would be here as well, in this place with the chubby black-haired baby he adored and the strange circumstances of that child's anguished mother and father.

He rocked back and forth, thinking about the

two people who had loved each other for a night and given to the world a little girl.

He rocked, and asked that there be peace for them all, and little pain.

Then, he let them go.

WHEN Dusky had emerged from the womb, covered with the blood and mucus of her mother's body, Anne remembered the skin of the baby's father and the salty slick sweat of it. She had reached for the baby and, before it was cleansed, laid it naked against her own bare body, celebrating in her heart the love that had created the child.

There was no bitterness in her toward the man who had mixed himself with her and created a black-haired little girl. Only a loneliness

*for him because now, Anne knew, she would not
have him at all. She would not have the long
white envelopes from his desk in New York, nor
the telephone calls which had arrived nearly always at nine-thirty Monday mornings, nor the
feel of his hand, the warmth of his lips as he
greeted her in the doorway of his office once
every year. He would not be there, across the
room at a cocktail party, for her eyes to devour
hungrily, memorizing each crease of his face,
the line of his back, the hair on his hands.*

*With the gift of Dusky, she had to give up
Ben.*

*He called her, again, exactly a year after she
had requested time apart, and only days after he
had spoken with Chip.*

*Anne did not know of that call between her
son and Ben, and Ben did not tell her. Only his
knowing of Dusky was important.*

*And he told her, immediately, that he knew.
He asked her then if she wanted him there, in
her life, with his child—a part of that home in
Seattle.*

*Anne had considered the inevitable pain for
many people should Ben want to live out his responsibility to his baby. And particularly she*

had considered the pain for herself—the viola-
tion of her privacy and her autonomy as the life
of Ben's family became intertwined with her
own. And because of this she knew, and told
him, that she did not want him with her. Not
today.

It was the response he had hoped for. Because
even if she had asked for his involvement, he
would have tried to change her mind. He was
not prepared to hurt so many by living out two
broken lives. Chip had confronted him already
with that terrible possibility.

He offered to send some money for Dusky,
and Anne accepted. Then they were faced with
goodbye.

To the surprise of them both, Ben began to
cry as he tried to express to Anne what she had
meant to him, and what the new child meant.
Each time he began to speak, his voice gave way
and instead he could only surrender to the
mourning.

Anne, too, cried. He knew how she loved him,
so there was no need of more revelation of that.
She asked him to wait on the line, then went
into the nursery, bringing Dusky back in her
arms.

Anne laid the sleeping infant up against her shoulder, the small face turned out toward the morning sun.

And knowing the baby was with them, Ben and Anne shared the soft sounds of their child and the quiet grieving of each other.

"Will you be all right?" he asked her.

"Yes."

And they parted.